Hare and Tortoise

Race to the Moon

An Aesop's fable retold
and illustrated by

Oliver J. Corwin

Harry N. Abrams, Inc.,
Publishers

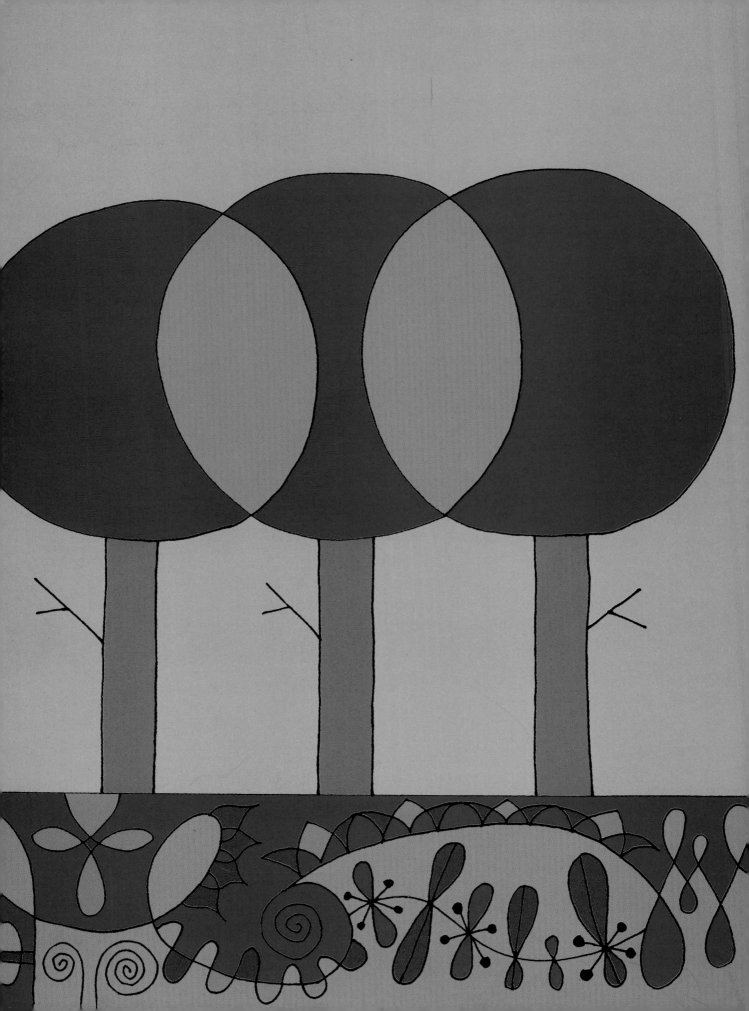

Although Tortoise and Hare had been best friends since they first met in school, Hare always teased Tortoise about being a super slowpoke.

One day, deciding enough was enough, Tortoise challenged Hare to race to the moon!

Hare had a lot of money and bought an aerodynamic hyperspaceship of the latest design.

Tortoise, on the other hand, had no money. He made a
spaceship all on his own, using whatever parts he could find.

Hare's spaceship was slick, shiny, and super-duper fast.

Tortoise's spaceship was rinky-dink and very, very slow.
Even Snail, who's slower than slow, laughed at Tortoise.

When they were ready, their friend Squirrel, as loud as he could, began the starting countdown . . .

"10 – 9 – 8 – 7 – 6 – 5 – 4 – 3 – 2 – 1 – BLAST OFF!"

Hare's spaceship engines rumbled like thunder.
Tortoise's just rattled and buzzed.

Tortoise's spaceship went putt, putt, putt.

VOOOSH!
Hare whizzed right by him.
"Woo-hoo, eat my dust!"
yelled Hare.

Hare's spaceship nearly knocked some birds clear out of the sky!
"I'm fast, fast, fast!" said Hare.

Tortoise's spaceship went putt, putt, putt.

"I'm so fast, I have all the time in the world!" said Hare to himself.
So he decided to make a few stops before going to the moon.

Hare quickly flew to the North Pole
and went sledding with a polar bear.
"Woo-hoo!" yelled Hare.

Then Hare, even more quickly, flew to the African plains, where the sun is very, very hot, and played cards with a friendly rhinoceros. "I wonder where that slowpoke Tortoise is right now?" said Hare.

Tortoise, super slow, but keeping on track, was already in the clouds. Putt, putt, putt.

"Keep on going, spaceship, ol' pal of mine!" said Tortoise.

Next, Hare soared to the rain forest, where he had a game of catch with a playful monkey.

Tortoise kept on track. Putt, putt, putt.

Hare finally decided to fly up through the clouds.
VOOOSH! VOOOSH! RUMBLE! RUMBLE!
But he stopped to take a nap. "I'm so fast, I have all the time in the world!" said Hare to himself. And boy, did he really snore!

Night came, and the stars lit the way.

Tortoise, super slow but keeping on track, was way past the clouds and had reached outer space. He looked out at the stars and smiled.

Hare finally woke up and set his
controls for outer space!
VOOOSH! VOOOSH!
RUMBLE! RUMBLE!

Tortoise was looking back at the tiny earth when he heard a noise.
Was that Hare in the distance catching up? Could it be?

Hare's hyperwarp-drive, deluxe engines rumbled with the speed of one thousand horses.

VOOOSH! VOOOSH! RUMBLE! RUMBLE!

Hare could see the moon. Hot dog!

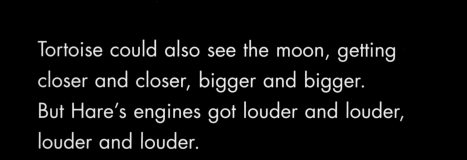

Tortoise could also see the moon, getting
closer and closer, bigger and bigger.
But Hare's engines got louder and louder,
louder and louder.

Then right before Hare pushed the special lever for a super-speedy
space travel landing, he heard...
RATTLE! TATTLE! CLANK! BANG!

Tortoise's landing gear! Hare watched as Tortoise floated
down through the bright light of the twinkling stars toward
the surface of the glowing moon.

Touchdown! A perfect landing. Even though he was super slow, and putt-putted along, Tortoise never gave up. He kept on track and finally won the race!

"Tortoise, you slowpoke, what are you doing here?" asked Hare after he landed last.

"Never mind that, Hare, you super-duper slowpoke," said Tortoise. "Use those hop-hopping feet and jump toward the stars with me. We can jump six times higher on the moon!"

And being best friends, that is exactly what they did.

For my parents and Amy

A special thanks to Howard Reeves, Becky Terhune, Emily Farbman, Juan Carlos Sobrino, Fabian Alsultany, Ana Carola Villacorta, and Lia Ronnen

Author's Note

My mother is an artist and with her encouragement, I came to love drawing at an early age. Growing up with my pets Herman and Jumper, respectively a tortoise and a rabbit, I have always had a special appreciation for the Aesop's tale, "The Hare and the Tortoise." Part of me is like Hare and another part is like Tortoise. Like Hare, I enjoy jumping from idea to idea, but the Tortoise part of me helps me to push myself to focus on and stick with one idea until it is fully developed. Effort brings an idea to reality. Recently, while looking at a sculpture based on the story, I wondered how it might have been different if told today for the first time — maybe a race to the moon!

I am inspired by traditional Moroccan art, modern design from the 1930s to the 1950s, and patterns. Patterns can convey energy, like rockets in flight; they can reflect tranquillity and beauty, like the stars in the sky; or they can be merely decorative. All these influences combine in my own work.

To create my art, I begin with the basic idea, and then start to draw pictures. These drawings help me to develop the story. After I have the story mapped out, I sketch the scenes with pencil and pen. Once they are tight drawings, I scan the images onto the computer. I then choose my palette and color the pieces digitally. I sometimes redo them again and again. With a little persistence, and by keeping on track, I achieve the final illustration.

—Oliver J. Corwin

Designer: Becky Terhune
Production Director: Hope Koturo

Library of Congress Cataloging-in-Publication Data
Corwin, Oliver J.
Hare and Tortoise race to the moon / retold and illustrated by Oliver J. Corwin.
p. cm.
Summary: Best friends Tortoise and Hare compete to see who will be first to reach the moon.
ISBN 0-8109-0566-3
[1. Turtles—Fiction. 2. Hares—Fiction. 3. Racing—Fiction. 4. Space
flight to the moon—Fiction.] I. Title.
PZ7.C816875 Har 2002
[E]-dc21
2001006463

Printed and bound in Hong Kong

10 9 8 7 6 5 4 3 2 1

Harry N. Abrams, Inc.
100 Fifth Avenue
New York, N.Y. 10011
www.abramsbooks.com

Abrams is a subsidiary of
LA MARTINIÈRE
GROUPE